T0380913

Model
Behavior

Charlotte

Nicole A. Davis

Illustrated by: Billy Pondexter Jr.

Interior Image Credit: Billy Pondexter Jr.

Scripture quotations taken from the New American Standard Bible® (NASB),
Copyright © 1960, 1962, 1963, 1968, 1971, 1972, 1973,
1975, 1977, 1995 by The Lockman Foundation
Used by permission. www.Lockman.org

WestBow Press books may be ordered through booksellers or by contacting:

WestBow Press
A Division of Thomas Nelson & Zondervan
1663 Liberty Drive
Bloomington, IN 47403
www.westbowpress.com
1 (866) 928-1240

ISBN: 978-1-9736-5055-3 (sc)
ISBN: 978-1-9736-5054-6 (e)

Library of Congress Control Number: 2019900227

Print information available on the last page.

WestBow Press rev. date: 01/15/2019

Charlotte

She stared at the bluish green water churning beneath her feet, mesmerized by the white caps breaking through the surface. Her white gown flapped around her legs in the sudden breeze and she gripped the railing behind her even harder to keep from falling in. Her heart beat within her chest faster and harder as she thought for the fifth time that this wasn't a good idea. *Why did I leave the prom?*

Then she remembered the smiling faces and laughing couples that danced in the banquet hall of the hotel room:

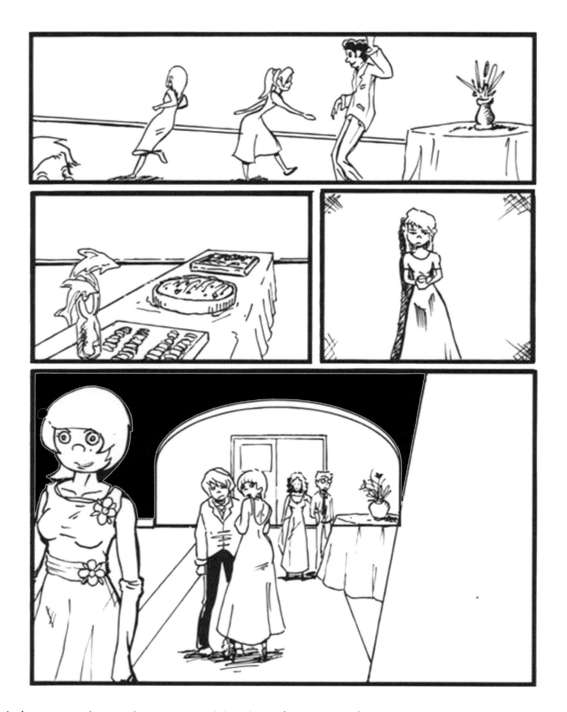

The lights were dimmed; an array of food, such as fried chicken wings, cocktail shrimp, spinach dip and pita chips, along with various cakes and chocolate desserts were laid out buffet style alongside the walls in order to keep the dance floor clear. The music rolled across the room in a rhythmic manner that she could feel inside her chest, almost beating with her heart. Couples laughed as they twirled on the dance floor; the diamond and jewel encrusted necklaces and bracelets of the girls glittered as they went by. And yet, she stood against the wall-watching. She longed to join the merry makers, but she did not know how to make herself get off the wall.

She hated them, their smiling faces, their laughter, if only someone would talk to her. As she stood watching, she was overcome with just how alone she really was. No one would notice if she left. No one would notice if she quietly slipped out, if she were to die. They wouldn't come to her funeral; they might not even know that she was dead until weeks later. All of this reminded her of why, months before, she had planned to kill herself on this very night.

In the secret drawer of her dresser was a list of her preparations. She'd had a long soak in a bathtub filled with lavender and rose scented soap. Carefully she had shaved her legs and applied makeup to her face. She then got dressed in the most beautiful prom dress she had ever seen: white with white lace along the sleeves and at the edges of the full skirt that spread out umbrella style. It reminded her of a wedding gown, which was appropriate, because tonight she planned on marrying death.

On the night stand at home was a full bottle of sleeping pills and a gallon of water neatly situated in front of a makeup mirror so she could watch her face as she downed each pill. That had been the plan. At the end of prom, she would go home, take the pills and fall into a never ending sleep. She had even written her suicide note; one line attached to the mirror on a sticky note- I'm sorry.

But plans change. While she was at the prom, staring at the young couples, her loneliness had never been as complete. She had no date, she had no friends, no one with whom she could "hang out" with. She blamed her military father for this. They were constantly moving and she never had an opportunity to really settle down and open up enough to make a friend. She knew her shyness was another large contributor to her friendlessness. She envied the girls who were so full of energy and confidence that they could talk to anyone they wanted.

An hour into the prom, her depression finally got to her. She didn't want to break down and cry in front of all the smiling faces, so she fled. She ran through the front lobby of the hotel and onto the street, tears streaming down her face; her heels making a strange click, scrch sound as she skidded pounded across the pavement.

She hadn't been paying attention to where she was going and drew up short at a bridge. It was a large bridge with two lanes and only a couple of yellow lines separating the two sides. The floor of the bridge was completely made of metal, and the stop light at the entrance indicated that it was a draw bridge.

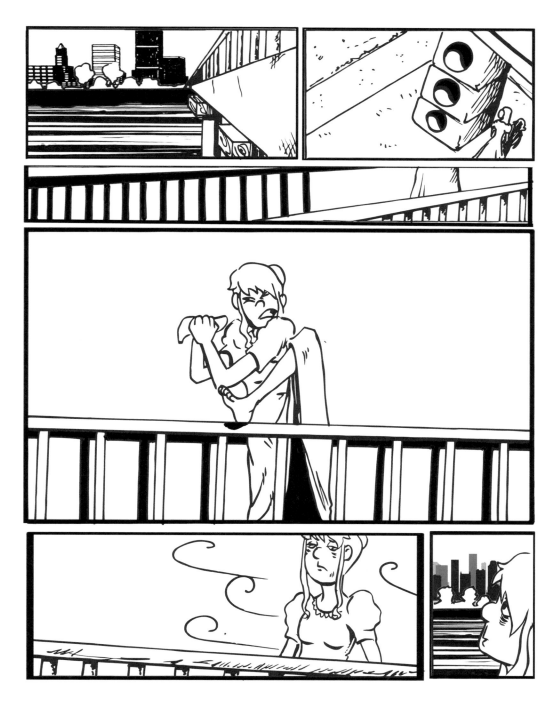

Beneath the bridge was a sea of water spanning a few miles in both directions from what she could see in the dim light.

On the left side of the bridge was a little ledge spanning the length of the bridge for pedestrians and cyclists. She stepped out onto this walkway but it wasn't long before one of her heels slipped through one of the many grooves on the bridge. The floor of the bridge was similar to a grate. She slipped the heels off her feet and continued walking across the bridge, which was at least a half a mile long.

She looked at the water as she walked; it was a good thirty feet below her. She liked the way the moon rays played across the dark waters beneath. It was a full moon and it brought childhood memories of werewolves changing under the light of a full moon. People often did strange things during a full moon.

When she was about halfway across the bridge, she stopped, staring at the water beneath. She then looked to her left and right and saw that she was completely alone on the bridge. She could not even hear the sound of a car in the distance. On impulse she dropped her shoes, grabbed the rail in front of her and lifted her leg across. It was difficult because her skirt snagged on the little edges and screws of the rail, but she managed to get one leg across, and placed her foot on the ledge.

When she tried to bring her other leg around, her skirt was in the way and she lost her footing. She screamed and wrapped both arms tightly around the railing, her heart beating within her throat. But when she didn't fall, she calmed down. Shifting her feet on the ledge and alternating her hands, she turned around and looked at the waters beneath, churning and writhing much like her stomach. It would be all too easy to just jump in. All she would have to do is let go; then it would all be over. All her misery, her loneliness, the sick feeling in her stomach when in a large crowd of people, or standing in front of class giving a speech, would be gone. She would drink as much of the water as she could to accelerate her drowning. She started to loose her fingers from the rail when she was startled by a shout behind her.

"Don't jump!" The voice startled her so much that she lost her footing and hung from the air, held only by her hands. She'd managed to turn so that her stomach was pressed against the bridge. Tears ran in rivulets down her cheeks as she sobbed in the air, staring at the water, into the face of death. She realized that she was not yet ready to die, but death was now ready for her. She cried, kicking her feet, trying to lift them back up to the ledge, but her skirt kept getting in the way and all she could do was hang. She heard scrambling above her head and then a warm hand was touching hers.

"Here, give me your hand."

"If I let go, I'll fall!" she sobbed.

"Alright, well swing your legs up to me, and we'll try to get you back on the ledge."

"Ok." She tried kicking her legs up, but couldn't manage a swing in her current position. "I can't do it!" Panic was settling in on her and she could feel her hands getting sweaty against the rough metal, any minute now she would drop.

"I'm going to lean over the railing, grab my arms and I'll pull you up."

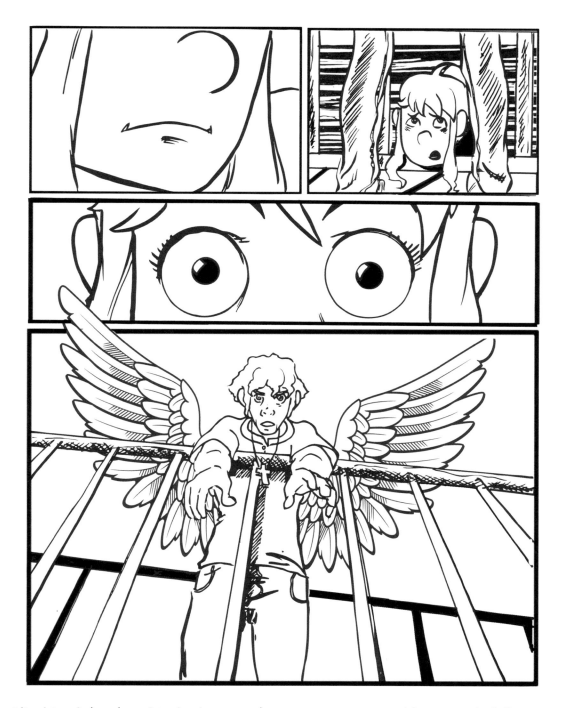

She tilted back her head to look up at this crazy person, and her mouth fell open.

An angel was leaning across the railing, his golden hair silhouetted by the moon light with his arms stretched out toward her. He grabbed both her arms by the biceps, and she quickly clasped her fingers behind his neck. He pulled her up by straightening his back and then wrapping his arms around her torso; he was able to bring her across the railing. She clung to him as if he were a pillow after a bad dream, or a man who had just saved her life, because he had.

He hugged her just as tightly, trying to comfort her, she thought. She sobbed on his shoulders for a few minutes, bathing him with her tears and snot from her nose, thinking incoherently that an angel had just saved her life. She was vaguely aware of his hands stroking her back and patting her hair, shh sssshhh noises coming out of his mouth as he told her she was okay. Abruptly she realized that he didn't have any wings and she stiffened. She jerked away from him, "You tried to kill me!"

She got to watch in satisfaction as his startled face turned to shock. He was really quite beautiful; delicate cheek bones enhanced by a strong chin. His golden curls stuck damply to his face; he was only a couple of years older than she was.

"Me?! Are you crazy?! What were you doing over the ledge?!"

"Getting a better look." She said stubbornly. Her eyes caught on a silver cross dangling from his neck. It was a plain cross with straight edges, but it seemed to glow in the moon light. His black shirt heightened this effect.

"Thank God you are alright." He dragged a shaky hand through his hair.

"Why would I thank him?" She stooped down and grabbed at her shoes that she had left on the ground when she climbed over the rail.

She glared at him as she raised her head.

He opened his mouth as if to say something, but closed it again. Not saying another word, she turned around and began walking in the direction from which she had come.

"Wait. Wait!" She heard running behind her, then a firm hand closed on her shoulder. "Where are you going?" he asked incredulously.

"Home," she tried to shrug his hand off.

"Well at least let me take you." She looked to where he pointed.

A black mustang was parked in the middle of the road, the driver side door open. She hadn't even heard him pull up. His was the only car on the road.

Without talking to him, she tossed her shoes over the railing leading to the main part of the bridge, then tried swinging her leg over. However, her skirts caught again and she almost landed on her face, but steadying arms grabbed her from behind.

He didn't let her go until her feet were firmly planted on the ground. Then he easily climbed over the railing himself. She watched him, curious as to how he looked underneath his clothes. She thought she could see his muscles bunch beneath the black collar shirt when he lifted himself over the railing. And although he wore jeans, she knew his legs would also be muscular.

She blushed when he looked at her and turned her face from him.

He ran to the car and pressed the unlock button on the drivers side door, and then went around to open the door for her. She heard the engine running as she got into the car. He hadn't even turned the car off before he went to save her.

"Where to?" he asked once he was behind the wheel. She looked at her hands, feeling shy. She wasn't sure of where she was, but she knew she did not want to go back to the hotel. She didn't want to go home either.

"Are you hungry?"

She nodded her head.

"Okay." He shifted the car into gear and began to drive. They rode in silence. She stared out the window and he concentrated on the road. She looked at the clock; it was a quarter past twelve. She'd been on the bridge for nearly an hour.

As he pulled into the parking lot of a twenty-four hour eatery, she began to cry.

"What's wrong?" She could hear the worry in his voice.

"I forgot my purse." She sniffled.

He smiled, squeezing her hand, "Don't worry about it."

It was when they walked into the restaurant that she remembered her tattered dress. She rushed off to the bathroom while he told the hostess they wanted a table for two. She was horrified at the sight she saw in the mirror. Her hair was a tangled bird's nest. She had black smudges all over her face where the mascara had run. Her white dress had patches of grey here and there and was torn.

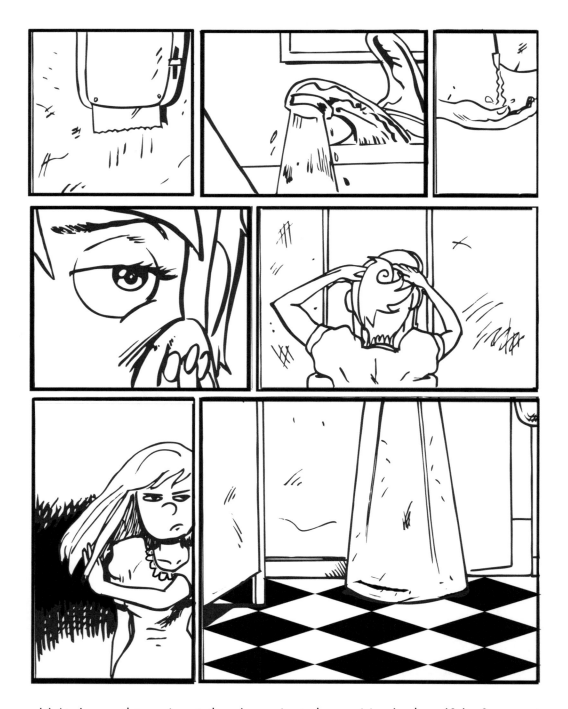

She couldn't do anything about the dress, but she grabbed a handful of paper towels, wet them and pumped some soap onto it. She scrubbed her face and then took out the multitudes of pins and hair bands that had held her hair in place. She combed out the tangled mass with her fingers. She didn't look like a princess anymore, but neither did she look like something the cat dragged in. Still, filled with embarrassment, she went to find him.

"There you are," he said as she crouched down into the booth, "I was beginning to worry." He sat straight up in his seat, tense.

"I was in the bathroom," she mumbled under her breath, looking at the table. The waitress asked them for their drink orders; they both asked for water.

"So," he drummed his fingers on the table, "so."

She could feel the awkwardness between them and it made her smile. This guy had just seen her at one of the worst moments of her life. He almost saw her commit suicide. She wondered if she had jumped, would he have jumped in after her.

But here they were, at a restaurant, about to get something to eat; the whole thing was so surreal.

"My name is Charlotte by the way," she reached out her hand in greeting; he shook it.

"Gabriel- Aww, don't frown like that, it's only a name." But he smiled knowingly.

"Why were you on the bridge anyway?" she asked him suspiciously.

He chuckled and leaned back in his chair, "You wouldn't believe me if I told you."

The waitress came back with their waters, but they weren't prepared to order and asked for a few more minutes.

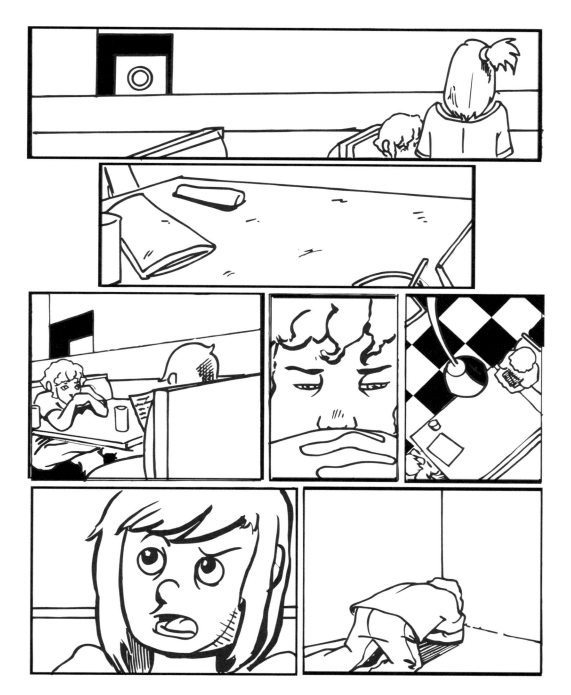

"Try me," she said, looking at the menu.

He sighed and put his menu down, then clasped his fingers, his elbows resting on the table. He looked at her until she too dropped her menu.

"God told me to go."

"What?" she looked at him in disbelief.

"I was at my house actually. Praying, the way I normally do around that time. When God told me that someone needed my help."

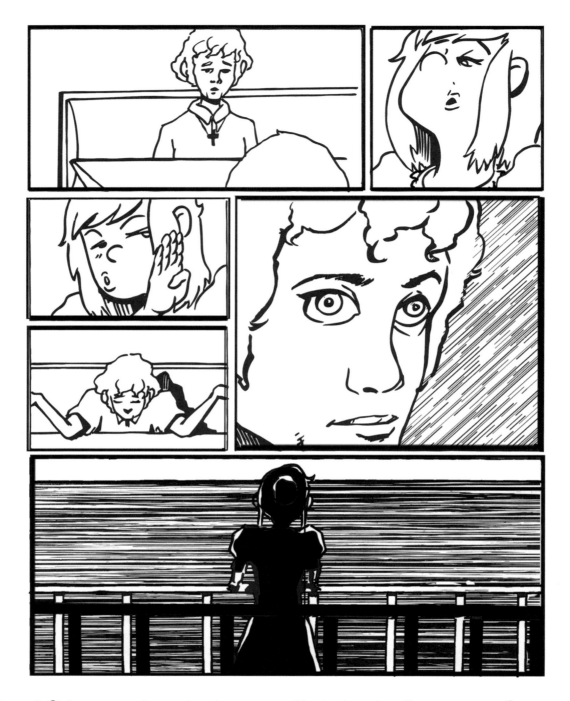

"Oh really?" her voice dripped with sarcasm. "And what did *God* sound like?"

He waved his hands as if to say *I knew you wouldn't believe me.*

"He doesn't exactly speak to me with words. At least not words I can hear. He speaks to my heart. He told me that someone needed me and I should drive down Hwy 1. I didn't even know what I was looking for. Seeing you was almost an accident. I had been fiddling with the radio and I just happened to glance up, and there you were."

Charlotte rolled her eyes and turned her head, but didn't say anything.

The waitress returned and they placed their orders. He ordered a steak with mashed potatoes and she asked for the cream cheese stuffed French toast.

"Why were you on the bridge?" he asked once the waitress was gone.

Charlotte shot him a dirty look.

He moved his hands in a calming manner, "I mean, I know why, but how did you get there? What made you decide to do that?"

Charlotte sat for a while, staring at the condensation on her glass of water, wondering if she should ignore him, or answer. Given the night's events, she decided to talk.

"Well, the bridge wasn't my plan. It just kind of happened. I was at my prom, and I just couldn't take it anymore. So I left. When I saw the bridge, I figured, why not?"

"What couldn't you take anymore?"

She looked at her hands, "The loneliness."

Gabriel nodded. "You-"

She interrupted him and spoke rapidly, "It's just, we move all the time. I don't have any friends, none, not even an acquaintance. My parents are never home. I'm all by myself. And I want to talk to people, I do. But I'm too shy; I don't know what to say. I don't know how to approach them."

She looked at him, her eyes pleading with him to understand. He nodded again.

"I get it, trust me. I've been there."

"Riiight," she sneered at him. "You're gorgeous. How could you not have friends?"

"Sure, I've had friends, if you want to call them that. I mean, they were people who would talk to me; we hung together, got high, whatever. But they didn't know me, and I didn't know them. It was more like an act. I couldn't really talk to them about any of the things that mattered to me. I couldn't talk to my parents. They are both doctors, so you can imagine how often they are home. We had a maid, but she barely spoke English. I had no one, or so I thought. I wanted to die."

At that moment the waitress appeared and gave him a strange look when she heard his last words. He blushed as she placed the plates in front of them, glancing over her shoulder at Gabriel as she walked away.

He chuckled; his head bent over his plate, and brushed some golden curls out of his face, "Oh God." He closed his eyes and placed his hands together. His lips began to move, but Charlotte couldn't hear what he said. When he finished with a quiet, "Amen," Charlotte asked, "So why didn't you?"

"Didn't I what?" He asked around a mouthful of steak.

"Why didn't you kill yourself?"

"Oh." He finished chewing and wiped his mouth on a napkin.

"Well, one day I was sitting at home, you know, flipping through the channels; and I saw this man on TV. It was one of those Christian preaching shows, or whatever. I don't even know why I stopped on it, but I did. And this man, this pastor was standing there and he started speaking to me. Just so you know, I was raised Catholic, but I didn't believe any of the garbage they were feeding me; but this man seemed to be the real deal."

"He said that we are all sinners; that even he sins. But although we sin, God loves us anyway. He said we all fall short of the glory of God; we can never be as perfect as he is. But God loves us so much that he sent his son, Jesus Christ, to die for our sins. Jesus is without sin, so the fact that a sinless man, this being, this *God*, was sent to earth, leaving all of his heavenly treasures behind to die, really spoke to me."

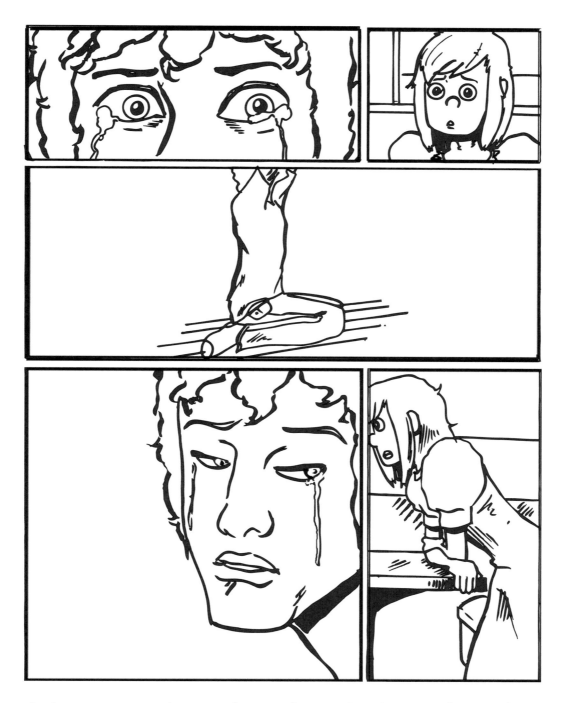

I mean, he loves me so much, so much more than my friends, so much more than my parents even, that he died for me so I wouldn't go to hell." Tears began leaking out of Gabriel's eyes, but he didn't seem to notice.

"So what did you do?"

"What could I do? I got on my knees and prayed like I haven't prayed in years. But I didn't do the ritualistic prayers they teach you in church, I prayed from my heart. I told God that I was tired of being disappointed by people, that I couldn't keep living my life the way I was, that I was tired of feeling alone. I told him that I needed him and the salvation Jesus Christ offers freely. I invited him to come into my life, to fill me with his love and to change the things within me that I could not change myself."

"Then what happened?" Charlotte was sitting on the edge of her seat, her food forgotten.

"He forgave me and accepted me as one of his own. After I accepted him into my life, he revealed his purpose for me. The purpose I had been ignoring all of these years," Gabriel said.

"So what's your purpose?"

"To love, serve, and glorify him. That's why I went to the bridge tonight, because my God called me to. The way he is calling you."

"Huh?" Charlotte looked at him confused, the hairs on the back of her neck standing up. She felt a tingling sensation start at the base of her neck and travel down her body until it was in her legs. Something told her that the next few words that came out of his mouth would be very important. Gabriel's face was serious, and he looked her directly in the eyes and did not break her gaze.

"God is calling you. He could have left you on that bridge. He could have let you jump, but he didn't. He sent me to rescue you because he has a purpose for you and your life. But ultimately the choice is yours; whether or not you want to follow him or continue to live your life the way you want."

Charlotte was stunned. No one had ever talked to her that way about life and God. She never thought she had a purpose in life, but that everything had all been a mistake. She always thought if someone had, she would laugh it off, or take it as a joke. But this moment, unlike so many moments in her life, was the most realist experience she ever had. This guy was sitting here, talking to her about herself, as if he knew her.

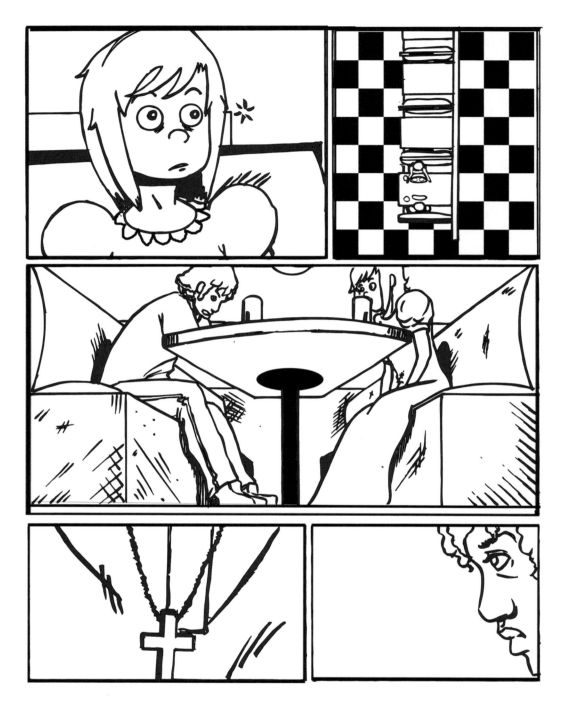

Gabriel continued, "You know, you are never alone. You may not be looking at God, but he's looking at you; waiting for you to call on him, waiting to call on you. He nor I can do it for you. It's something you have to decide for yourself. And you know what, it can be scary; but not as scary as life can be without him. When I walk through life I want to know that God is with me, ordering my steps. I don't want to think that one day he'll say, *ok, have it your way* and let me go; because on that day I will be truly lost. I know that without God I have no security."

"Everything and anything bad can happen to me; a car accident, a shot in the dark, one of the other horrible things that life seems to throw at us. But with God I don't have to be afraid; he will get me through anything. I have the security and assurance of my Lord Jesus. I know that all things in my life will work for good. I have nothing to fear. I don't even fear death. Because I know when I die I will go to heaven and be with him. What's to fear?"

Charlotte nodded, "You have a lot of confidence."

"Yeah," Gabriel took a sip of water, and this time Charlotte caught his eye.

"What do I have to do to gain such confidence?"

Gabriel put down his cup and returned her look.

"The Bible says if you confess with your mouth and believe in your heart that Jesus Christ died on the cross and rose from the dead to save you from your sins, then you too will be saved."

Charlotte took a deep breath and asked him one more question, "Will you help me?"
"That's why I'm here."

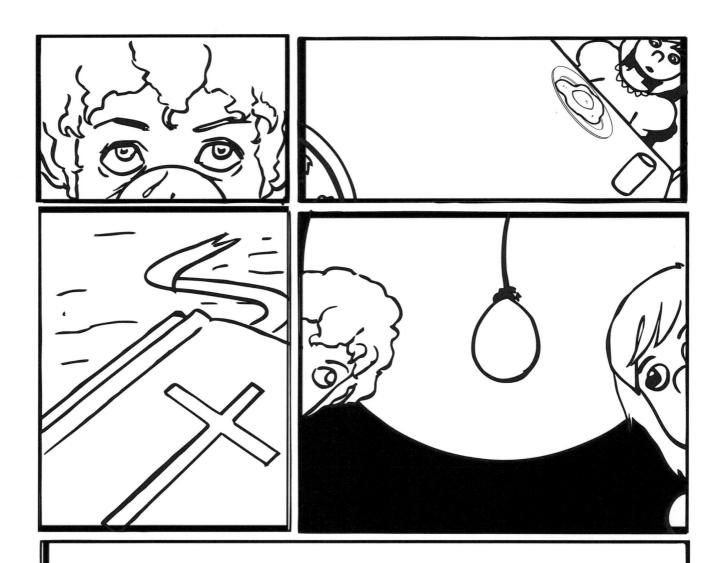

Romans 10:9-11:

If you confess with your mouth Jesus as Lord, and believe in your heart

that God raised Him from the dead, you will be saved; for with the heart a person

believes, resulting in righteousness, and with the mouth he confesses, resulting in

salvation. For the Scripture says, "WHOEVER BELIEVES IN HIM WILL NOT

BE DISAPPOINTED."

Printed in the United States
By Bookmasters